TONY CRUNK
BIG MAMA

Pictures by Margot Apple

Farrar, Straus and Giroux • New York

For Allison and for West Side —T.C.

For Tony and Ms. Vada Nevels —M.A.

Text copyright © 2000 by Tony Crunk
Pictures copyright © 2000 by Margot Apple
All rights reserved
Distributed in Canada by Douglas & McIntyre Ltd.
Color separations by Hong Kong Scanner Arts
Printed and bound in the United States of America by Worzalla
Typography by Rebecca A. Smith
First edition, 2000

Library of Congress Cataloging-in-Publication Data
Crunk, Tony.
   Big Mama / Tony Crunk ; pictures by Margot Apple. — 1st ed.
      p.   cm.
   Summary: Billy Boyd likes living with his grandmother, Big Mama,
because she can make a space capsule out of junk, joins in all kinds
of games, and turns a trip for ice cream into an adventure.
   ISBN 0-374-30688-5
   [1. Grandmothers—Fiction.] I. Apple, Margot, ill. II. Title
PZ7.C88955Bi   2000
[E]—dc21   99-34557

Big Mama is Billy Boyd's grandmother.
His grandfather's name is Papa.
Billy Boyd lives with them
because he doesn't have
a mother or father anymore.

Big Mama lets us do everything.

At Big Mama's house, you don't have to worry
about the screen door slamming behind you,
or about which glass you can take outside,
or about what else you can put
on your jelly sandwich besides jelly.

At Big Mama's house, you can camp out in the living room.
You can play submarine around her kitchen table.
You can crawl to the center of the earth under the back porch.

Big Mama can build a freight train
out of some chairs and an old sheet.

She can make a space capsule or a mule wagon
out of a grocery box and some planks.

If you are playing Time Travel
you can talk backward to her, in intergalactic code,
and she never says, "You children stop acting so silly."
Usually she starts talking backward, too.

If you need something, like a paper clip
or a piece of string or a pop-bottle top,
Big Mama has it in her housecoat pocket.

Big Mama is a good kickball player, too.
Well, pretty good.
She can kick it real far,

but she can't run very fast,
so usually she gets tagged out anyway.

Once, we were having a dirt-clod fight,
and we broke out Mrs. Todd's kitchen window.
Big Mama went with us to help us explain.

But then she made us mow Mrs. Todd's yard
all the rest of the summer.
For free.

Sometimes, when we come over after supper,
Big Mama gives us jars
with holes punched in the lids
to catch lightning bugs.

Papa counts up how many we catch
and gives a nickel to whoever has the most.
Then Big Mama helps us turn them all loose,
back out into the night.

But, best of all, sometimes on late afternoons
Big Mama takes us all down to Woody's for ice cream.
Woody's is only a few blocks away,
but it takes us forever to get there.

Big Mama gives each one of us fifty cents
from her big black pocketbook
and says, "Let's go, children,"
and we start out walking . . .

down Simpson's alley,
for some hide-and-seek,

along by Mrs. Grooms's corn patch,
where we help pull weeds from the garden,

around the corner, by Mr. Young's mule barn,
to visit Coot and Henrietta,

down McPherson Avenue,
to watch the road crew at work,

quick past Mickey Tucker's house,
where some of the tough kids hang out,

then along by Mr. Chester's junkyard,
to see what new treasures he has,

stopping at the corner of Third and Fowler,
to wave to Papa on his way home,

down by Mrs. Tuggle's vegetable stand,
just in time to help her put away her baskets
for the day . . .

coming out, finally, in front of Woody's.

Big Mama tells us when to run across the street.
Then she stands at the window
and makes sure Woody gets our orders right.

But the very best part is going back . . .
back by Mrs. Tuggle's vegetable stand,

back along by Mr. Chester's junkyard,
back past Mickey Tucker's,

back around Mr. Young's mule barn,
back by Mrs. Grooms's corn patch,
back up Simpson's alley . . .

crickets chirring in the yards,
white moths flitting around the streetlamps,

Big Mama out in front
swinging her big black pocketbook—

Big Mama leading us all home.